W9-BPP-477

5/20/05

Author's Note

While I have tried to make the transliterations and pronunciations of every number in this book as accurate as possible by consulting dictionaries and native speakers, subtleties in individual languages were not always able to be completely translated.

Library of Congress Cataloging-in-Publication Data

Evans, Lezlie.
Can you count ten toes?: count to 10 in 10 different languages / Lezlie Evans; Illustrated by Denis Roche.
p.   cm.
Summary: Rhyming verses instruct the reader to count different objects in one of ten languages, including Spanish, Japanese, Russian, Tagalog, and Hebrew.
RNF ISBN: 0-395-90499-4   PAP ISBN: 0-618-49487-1
1. Counting—Juvenile literature.   [1. Counting. 2. Polyglot materials.] I. Roche, Denis, ill. II. Title.
QA113.E84   1999
513.2'11—dc21   97-48915CIP AC

Manufactured in China
SCP 10 9 8 7 6 5

For my father, Gordon Peterson, a truly wonderful man —
whom I can always count on.
— L.E.

For Daisy Scarlett
— D.R.

CAN YOU COUNT TEN TOES?

Count to 10 in 10 Different Languages

Lezlie Evans   *Illustrated by* **Denis Roche**

Houghton Mifflin Company
Boston

Can you count ten toes, ten toes?
Count them if you please.
Count the toes from one to ten,
but count in **Japanese.**

❶ **いち** ichi (ee-chee)

❷ **に** ni (nee)

❸ **さん** san (sahn)

❹ **し** shi (she)

❺ **ご** go (go)

❻ **ろく** roku (roe-koo)

❼ **しち** shichi (she-chee)

❽ **はち** hachi (ha-chee)

❾ **きゅう** ku (koo)

❿ **じゅう** ju (joo)

Can you count the orbs in space,
nine planets plus the sun?
Try to speak in **Russian** as
you count them one by one.

1 **один** odin (ah-DEEN)

2 **два** dva (dvah)

3 **три** tri (tree)

4 **четыре** chetyre (chih-TIR-ee)

5 **пять** pyat (pyat)

6 **шесть** shest (shayst)

7 **семь** sem (syem)

8 **восемь** vosem (VOH-syem)

9 **девять** devyat (DYEH-vit)

10 **десять** desyat (DYEH-sit)

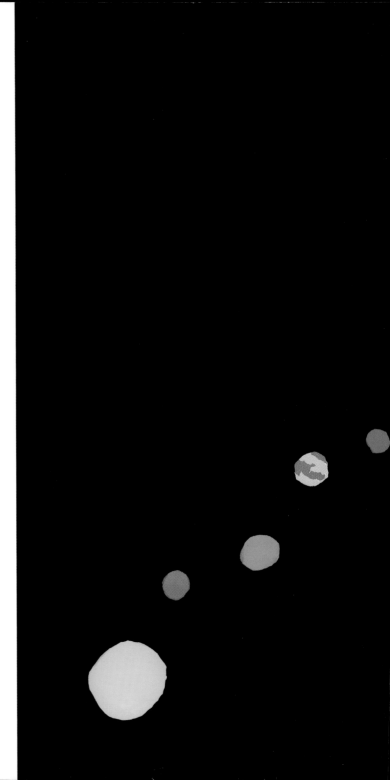

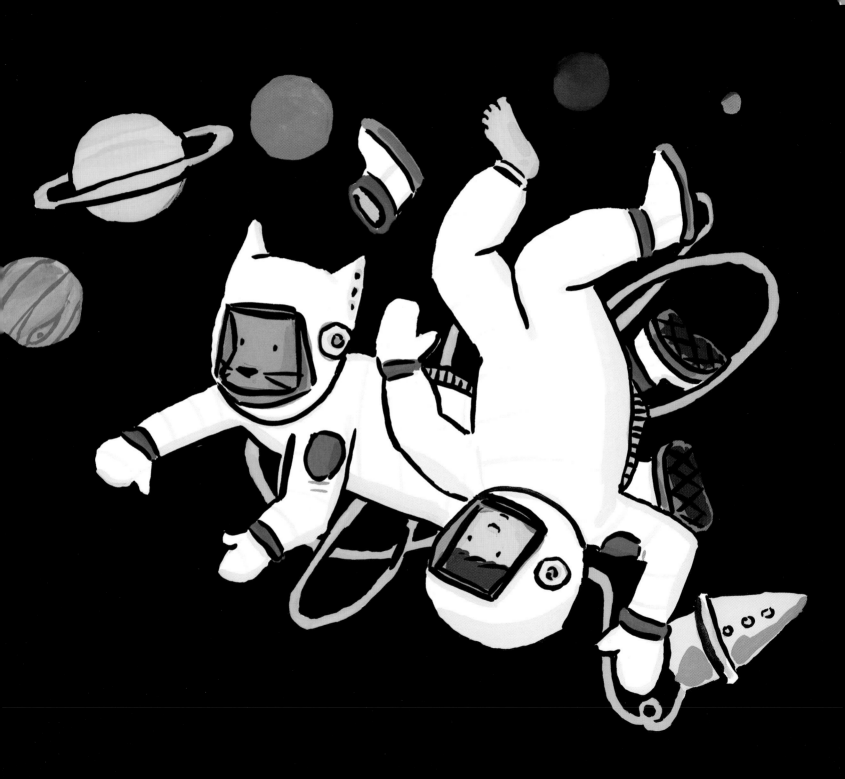

Can you count the angelfish
swimming in the sea?
You can speak **Korean** as you
count them, one, two, three.

1 **하나** hana (HA-nah)

2 **둘** tul (tool)

3 **셋** set (set)

4 **넷** net (net)

5 **다섯** tasot (TAH-sut)

6 **여섯** yosot (YUH-sut)

7 **일곱** ilgop (ILL-gup)

8 **여덟** yodol (YUH-dul)

9 **아홉** ahup (AH-hope)

10 **열** yol (yul)

Can you count the different coins
spread across the table?
Speaking now in **Zulu**, try to
count them, if you're able.

1 **kunye** (koo-NYAH)

2 **kubili** (koo-BEE-lee)

3 **kuthathu** (koo-TAH-too)

4 **kune** (koo-NEH)

5 **kuhlanu** (koo-THA-noo)

6 **isithupha** (ee-see-TOO-pa)

7 **isikhombisa** (ee-see-kom-BEE-sa)

8 **shiyagalombili** (she-ya-ka-lom-BEE-lee)

9 **shiyagalolunye** (she-ya-ka-lon-LOON-yeh)

10 **shiumi** (SHOE-me)

Can you count the ten balloons
floating in the sky?
Count each one, but count in **French**
before they pass you by!

 **un** (uhn)

2 **deux** (duh)

3 **trois** (twah)

4 **quatre** (kat)

5 **cinq** (sank)

6 **six** (seece)

7 **sept** (set)

8 **huit** (weet)

9 **neuf** (nuhf)

10 **dix** (deece)

Can you count the different hats
hanging on the wall?
As you count in **Hindi**, please
be sure to count them all.

1 १ **ek** (ache)

2 २ **do** (doe)

3 ३ **tin** (teen)

4 ४ **char** (char)

5 ५ **panch** (ponch)

6 ६ **chha** (chay)

7 ७ **sat** (sot)

8 ८ **ath** (ahrt)

9 ९ **nau** (now)

10 १० **das** (duss)

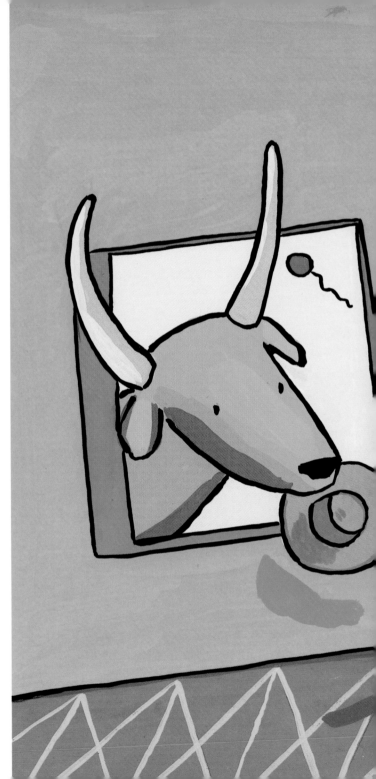

Count the children on the bus,
count them, one, two, three.
Speak now in **Tagalog** as
you count each child you see.

1 **isa** (ee-SAH)

2 **dalawa** (dah-lah-WAH)

3 **tatlo** (taht-LOH)

4 **apat** (AH-paht)

5 **lima** (lee-MAH)

6 **anim** (AH-neem)

7 **pito** (pee-TOH)

8 **walo** (wah-LOH)

9 **siyam** (see-YAHM)

10 **sampu** (sahm-POH)

Can you count ten different boats floating in the bay?
Count each one in **Hebrew** now before they sail away.

① אחת **achat** (ah-KHOT)

② שתיים **shtayim** (SHTY-eem)

③ שלוש **shalosh** (sha-LOSH)

④ ארבע **arba** (ar-BAH)

⑤ חמש **chamesh** (khah-MAYSH)

⑥ שש **shesh** (shaysh)

⑦ שבע **sheva** (sheh-VAH)

⑧ שמונה **shmone** (shmo-NEH)

⑨ תשע **tesha** (TAY-shah)

⑩ עשר **eser** (ES-sair)

Can you count the lightning bugs?
Quick, before they vanish!
Count each bug from one to ten,
saying it in **Spanish.**

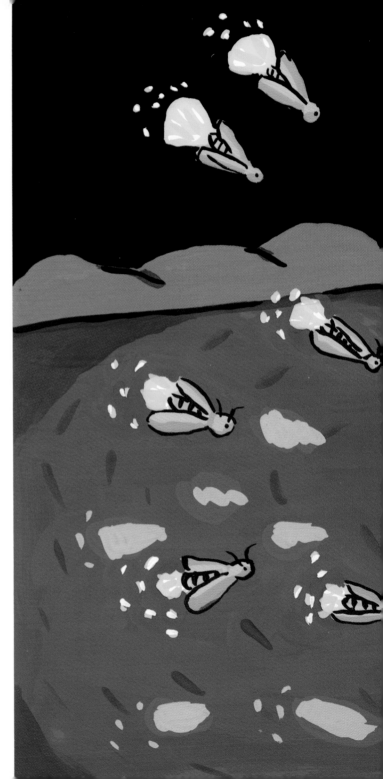

 **uno** (OO-no)

2 **dos** (dose)

3 **tres** (trace)

4 **cuatro** (KWA-tro)

5 **cinco** (SING-ko)

6 **seis** (sace)

7 **siete** (see-EH-tay)

8 **ocho** (O-cho)

9 **nueve** (NWEH-vay)

10 **diez** (DEE-es)

Can you count each country's flag
waving in the breeze?
Try to count them one by one,
but count them in **Chinese.**

1 一 **yi** (ee)

2 二 **er** (are)

3 三 **san** (sahn)

4 四 **si** (suh)

5 五 **wu** (woo)

6 六 **liu** (leo)

7 七 **qi** (chee)

8 八 **ba** (bah)

9 九 **jiu** (jeo)

10 十 **shi** (shr)

Now you've counted one through ten
in many different tongues,
but no matter how you say it
counting can be fun!

Can you count each colored dot?
Count them one by one.
Spot them all and you will learn
where they speak each tongue.

Chinese (Mandarin)
- ❶ China
- ❷ Taiwan
- ❸ Singapore

Hindi
- ❹ India

Hebrew
- ❺ Israel

Japanese
- ❻ Japan

Tagalog
- ❼ Philippines

Russian
- ❽ Russia

Zulu
- ❾ South Africa

Korean
- ❿ North Korea
- ⑪ South Korea

Spanish
- ⑫ Spain
- ⑬ Mexico
- ⑭ Colombia
- ⑮ Argentina
- ⑯ Chile
- ⑰ Cuba
- ⑱ Dominican Republic
- ⑲ Equatorial Guinea
- ⑳ Ecuador
- ㉑ Venezuela
- ㉒ Costa Rica
- ㉓ Nicaragua
- ㉔ Honduras
- ㉕ Guatemala
- ㉖ Panama
- ㉗ El Salvador
- ㉘ Peru
- ㉙ Bolivia
- ㉚ Paraguay
- ㉛ Uruguay

French
- ㉜ France
- ㉝ Belgium
- ㉞ Switzerland
- ㉟ Canada
- ㊱ Haiti
- ㊲ Monaco
- ㊳ Benin
- ㊴ Burkina Faso
- ㊵ Burundi
- ㊶ Cameroon
- ㊷ Central African Republic
- ㊸ Chad
- ㊹ Republic of the Congo
- ㊺ Côte d'Ivoire
- ㊻ Djibouti
- ㊼ Gabon
- ㊽ Guinea
- ㊾ Luxembourg
- ㊿ Madagascar
- 51 Mauritania
- 52 Niger
- 53 Rwanda
- 54 Senegal
- 55 Seychelles
- 56 Togo
- 57 Democratic Republic
  of the Congo

Here are some of the countries in which
these languages are officially spoken.